D0091879

# Betty the Bearded Dragon

by Debbi Michiko Florence

illustrated by Melanie Demmer

PICTURE WINDOW BOOKS
a capstone imprint

Thank you, Dow Phumiruk, for sharing stories about your rescue
bearded dragon, Sparkles — DMF

My Furry Foster Family is published by
Picture Window Books, a Capstone imprint
1710 Roe Crest Drive, North Mankato, Minnesota 56003
www.capstonepub.com

**Library of Congress Cataloging-in-Publication Data**
Names: Florence, Debbi Michiko, author.
Title: Betty the bearded dragon / by Debbi Michiko Florence.
Description: North Mankato, Minnesota : Capstone Press, [2020] |
Series: My furry foster family | Audience: Age 5–7. |
Audience: K to Grade 3.
Identifiers: LCCN 2019004828| ISBN 9781515844761 (library binding) |
ISBN 9781515845591 (paperback) | ISBN 9781515844808 (eBook PDF)
Subjects: LCSH: Bearded dragons (Reptiles) as pets—Anecdotes—
Juvenile literature. | Foster care of animals—Juvenile literature.
Classification: LCC SF459.L5 F56 2020 | DDC 639.3/955—dc23
LC record available at https://lccn.loc.gov/2019004828

Designer: Lori Bye

Photo Credits: Mari Bolte, 69; Melanie Demmer, 71; Roy Thomas, 70

Printed in the United States of America.
102019   000108

# Table of Contents

Dad
(Tim Takano)

Mom
(Cindy Takano)

Me
(Kaita Takano)

Eraser

Ollie

Joss Lawrence,
Happy Tails
Rescue

Hannah Miller,
my best friend

# CHAPTER 1

# Kaita Knows All

The school bus pulled up to my stop. I waved goodbye to my friends and stepped off. Mom and Ollie were waiting for me.

"Hi, Mom! Hi, Ollie!" I said. I gave my mom a hug. Then I patted my mini dachshund on his head.

*Yip! Yip! Yip!* Ollie was always happy to see me.

Mom handed Ollie's leash to me, and the three of us headed home. Ollie trotted in front. I loved how he held his tail high.

"How was your day today, Kaita?" Mom asked.

"Great!" I said. "You'll never guess what Mrs. Werner told the class. She said I'm an animal expert!"

"An expert, huh?" Mom said. She looked at me and winked.

"OK, maybe I'm not an *expert*," I said. "I have really learned a lot, though, since last year."

"Yes, we've *all* learned a lot," Mom said. "I'm glad we decided to foster animals."

Foster families like mine take care of pets that don't have forever homes. Sometimes people move away and can't take their pets along. Some people have allergies. We take care of the animals until new families can adopt them.

We work with Happy Tails Rescue. They help homeless animals. We adopted Ollie from them last year. That's how we decided to become a foster family. Fostering is hard work, but I love to help animals.

When we got home, Mom put her hand on my shoulder. Her eyes twinkled. "Kaita, I have a special surprise for you," she said. "Go check the guest room."

"Is it a new foster pet?" I asked. I took off my shoes, dropped my backpack in the hallway, and ran to the guest room.

*Yip! Yip! Yip!* Ollie chased after me. He wanted to see the surprise too!

I stopped in the guest room doorway. A huge glass tank sat on the table. It had a screened lid. A metal lamp rested on top, off to the side. Inside the tank were a rock, a branch, and two small bowls. A special carpet covered the bottom of the tank.

I didn't know what kind of animal was in there. I *did* know it wasn't a dog or a cat!

I walked up to the tank. Some sort of creature stood on the rock. "Whoa!" I said when I saw it. "It looks like a mini dragon!"

Mom laughed. "Close! It's a type of lizard called a bearded dragon. Her name is Betty."

"She's so cool!" I said. I pressed my face to the glass.

Betty was sand-colored, with brown spots. She had bumpy scales. Pointy spikes stuck out under her chin and along her sides. She stood on the rock, her head raised toward the lamp.

I wiggled my fingers in a wave. "Hi, Betty. My name's Kaita," I said.

Betty didn't turn her head, but her eye swiveled to look at me. Awesome!

"I think this is going to be a very fun adventure," Mom said. "Betty will be our family's first non-furry foster pet!"

I was happy to have a new foster pet. Betty seemed pretty amazing already. The problem was, I didn't know anything about bearded dragons.

The woman at Happy Tails Rescue, Joss, usually tells us what kind of animal we will foster. Then Mom brings home books from the bookstore so we can learn how to take care of it.

"Mom, did you know Betty was coming?" I asked.

"Not until today," Mom said. "Joss called me a couple of hours ago. A family dropped off Betty this morning. The kids didn't have time to play with her anymore."

"Oh. That's sad," I said.

Mom nodded. "At least they want her to find a good home," she said. "Joss doesn't have room for Betty at her house, so she called me. I told her we'd be happy to help."

"I don't know anything about bearded dragons. I don't know anything about lizards at all!" I said, worried.

Earlier today Mrs. Werner had called me an animal expert. I sure didn't feel like one anymore. How would I take good care of Betty?

# CHAPTER 2

# Meet Betty

Mom saw and heard how worried I was. "It'll be OK, Kaita," she said. She pointed to a folder on the desk. "Joss brought us some papers to read. She gave me some good tips too."

I still wished I had been able to learn about bearded dragons before Betty came. "I don't even know what the lamp does," I said.

"Well, this special lamp does two things," Mom said. "First, Betty needs to get vitamins from sunlight. The lamp acts like the sun. Second, all lizards are ectotherms." Mom smiled at me. "Do you know what that word means?"

"I do! She can only warm up or cool down from her surroundings," I said.

Ollie wagged his tail. It was like he knew I had the right answer.

"People are different," I continued. I looked down at Ollie. "Dogs are too. *Our* bodies keep us warm or cool us off from the *inside*."

"Right," Mom said. "Betty is basking under the lamp because it gives off heat like the sun. It warms her up. When she needs to cool down, she goes to the shady side of her tank."

Ollie pawed at my leg. I lifted him up so he could see Betty too. He sniffed around the tank lid.

"Why don't we give Betty some alone time?" Mom said. "We'll let her get used to her new home. Let's go have a snack!"

On my way out of the room, I grabbed the folder from Joss. I had some reading to do.

In the kitchen Ollie crunched his treats. I ate my yogurt and read about lizards. I did my homework. Then I played with Ollie in our backyard. I threw his ball, and he ran after it. He brought it back, and I tossed it again.

I thought about everything I had read from Joss' folder.

Bearded dragons eat fresh vegetables such as cabbage, kale, and carrots. They also eat live bugs. The first part was easy. Mom grew veggies in her garden. We could buy more at the market too. What about the live bugs, though? Would I have to catch them? How would I do that?

While Ollie chased a squirrel, I crawled under a bush. I looked on the leaves: no bugs. I dug in the dirt: only a few beetles. I worried about finding the right food for Betty.

Later I helped Mom start dinner. I made the salad. I tore up lettuce leaves and put them in a big bowl. I tossed in green beans, peppers, and sliced carrots.

I put some greens in a bowl for Betty too. Just as I was about to ask Mom about the bugs for Betty, Ollie barked.

*Yip! Yip! Yip!* Ollie dashed to the back door. Dad was home! I ran to hug him.

"Hello, Kaita! I hear we have a new foster pet," Dad said. He took off his shoes and jacket.

"We do! Her name is Betty, and she's a bearded dragon!" I said.

I tugged on Dad's arm. I was so excited to show him. I dragged him from the kitchen to the guest room.

Dad chuckled. "OK, OK, slow down, Kaita. I'm coming," he said.

Betty wasn't on the rock anymore. Now she was sitting on the branch, away from the lamp.

"She must have needed to cool off," I said. I turned to Dad. "Mom said I had to wait to take Betty out until you got home. She said it was really important that I wait for you. I don't know why, though."

"Well . . . I had a bearded dragon when I was in college," Dad said, smiling.

"You did?" I said. "Cool!"

This news was perfect! I bounced up and down on my toes. Dad would be the expert on Betty. I could learn all about bearded dragons from him.

Dad lifted the lid off the tank. "Joss said that Betty is used to being handled and is friendly," he said. "You should still be careful not to move too fast around her. She could scare easily."

I watched as Dad reached into the tank. He moved slowly and made sure Betty saw him. He carefully lifted her out. She stayed very still.

"You are a sweet beardie, aren't you?" Dad said to Betty.

"A what?" I giggled. "That sounds funny!"

"A beardie. That's what owners call their bearded dragons," Dad said.

"Oh. Then I guess it's kind of cute," I said. "Can I pet her?"

"Sure," Dad said.

I gently petted Betty's nose with my finger. "She feels dry and smooth. She feels warm too," I said.

I moved my finger to the little spines on her sides. "The spines look sharp and pokey, but they're soft and bendy."

I moved my finger back to her nose. I petted her some more. Betty closed her eyes.

"I think she likes you," Dad said.

Fostering Betty was going to be so much fun. I was happy she was here. I was even happier that Dad knew about beardies! I couldn't wait to learn more about them and tell my best friend, Hannah.

# CHAPTER 3

# Besties and Beardies

The next morning Hannah came over to see our newest foster pet. It was Saturday, so we had the whole day to hang out together.

"She's so pretty!" Hannah said.

Dad took Betty out of her tank and set her on the futon. Hannah and I sat on the floor. We were eye-level with the bearded dragon.

I showed Hannah how to pet Betty on her nose and along her head and back.

"I really like her," Hannah said. "What does she eat?"

"Bearded dragons eat mostly vegetables and live bugs," I said.

"Live bugs!" Hannah said. "How do you catch them?"

I smiled. That's what I had worried about yesterday. "I thought I had to catch them too," I said. "Then Dad told me that pet stores sell worms and crickets."

Dad held up a small cardboard box. "We bought some wax worms last night," he said.

Hannah jumped up. "Can I feed Betty?" she asked.

Hannah is my best friend, so I was happy to share Betty with her. "Let's both feed her," I said.

Dad put the wax worms in our hands. They were small, wiggly, and waxy white.

"They kind of tickle," Hannah giggled.

I put my hand in front of Betty. Her eyes turned down. She watched the wiggling worms. Quicker than I could blink, her fat pink tongue popped out. She slurped up one worm . . . then another . . . and another. *Slurp! Slurp! Slurp!*

"Wow!" Hannah said. "My turn!" She picked up one of the worms between her finger and thumb. She waved it in front of Betty.

Betty's tongue popped out and grabbed it. *Slurp!*

Hannah fed Betty the rest of her worms one by one.

When the worms were gone, I asked Dad if I could hold Betty.

"Sure," he said.

Hannah and I slowly moved from the floor to the futon. I gently scooped up Betty with both hands and put her on my lap. Betty looked at me for a few seconds. Then she started to climb me, like I was a tree!

Betty's tiny claws poked me as she gripped my shirt. I stayed very still. I couldn't stop a big smile from bursting across my face.

When Betty reached my shoulder, she stopped. Her head was next to my ear. Her tail hung down like a scarf.

"Ohhhh," Hannah said. She stared at Betty. I knew that look.

"Do you want to hold her?" I asked my best friend.

Hannah grinned. She nodded so hard that her ponytail bounced. I pulled Betty away from my shoulder and placed her on Hannah's lap.

Betty looked around, her eyes swiveling. She stared at Hannah for a bit, then started climbing up her shirt!

"Betty's old family must have carried her on their shoulders. She feels safe there," Dad said with a smile. "Well, you two have fun. I'll be in the other room if you need me."

After Dad left I said to Hannah, "I have an idea."

I brought in my doll stroller from the garage. We put Betty in it.

We slowly wheeled Betty through the house. We pretended she was the queen. We were taking her on a tour of her kingdom.

Queen Betty seemed to like it! She sat up tall. Her eyes moved up, down, and all around. Hannah and I took turns pushing the stroller. We had so much fun!

At lunchtime Dad put Betty back in her tank. She went right to the rock under the heat lamp. She really looked like a queen on a throne.

Hannah pressed her face against the glass and smiled. "Kaita, I think Betty is the best!" she said.

# CHAPTER 4

# The Clean Queen

The next day, when Dad let her out of her tank, Betty raced over to the stroller. The queen wanted a ride! I happily pushed her around the house.

Ollie trotted next to me like we were on a walk. Mom and Dad bowed when the three of us rolled by. We all laughed. Betty was the best, just like Hannah had said.

"Kaita, let's clean Betty's tank today and give her a bath," Dad said.

"She can take a bath?" I asked.

Mom nodded. "It's a good way to keep her healthy," she said.

Betty sat in the doll stroller and watched while Mom and Dad cleaned out her tank. They took out the rock and branch and scrubbed them. They took out the special carpet and washed it. Once everything was dry, I put it all back in the tank.

"Perfect! What do you think, Betty?" I asked.

Betty turned her head.

"Is it time for your bath now?" I asked.

"Time for Betty's bath," Mom said.

I rolled Betty into the bathroom. "Whoever adopts Betty has to have a stroller like this one," I said. She really seemed to like it!

"We'll make sure to check," Mom said.

Dad put down towels on the bathroom floor. "Beardies' claws make it tough for them to move on slippery surfaces," he said. "We'll make it easier for Betty with these towels."

"While you two give Betty a bath, I'm going to weed my garden," Mom said. "I'll take Ollie outside with me."

I lifted Betty out of the stroller and set her down on the towels. She looked around the bathroom. Her eyes swiveled. I loved how her eyes moved! She took a step forward and then another. She looked very queenlike as she walked. She held her chest and head high. Her tail swished back and forth.

Dad got a shallow plastic pan and put it in the bathtub. He filled it with warm water, just enough to reach Betty's chest.

When Dad placed her in the pan, she just sat there. Then . . . *zip, zip, zip!*

Betty raced around her little pool, splashing water everywhere! Dad and I both got wet. We started laughing.

When Betty heard us laugh, she stopped. She looked at us and opened her mouth wide. It looked like she was laughing too!

After bath time was over, I patted Betty dry. I put her back in her stroller.

"That went well," Dad said, picking up the towels. "Betty seems to feel safe with us. If you want to play with her in your room, Kaita, give it a try."

My eyes got big. "You mean, let her loose in my room?" I asked.

"Sure. See what she does," Dad said. "I think she'll be fine. Just take things slow. Let me know if you have any trouble."

So I rolled Betty to my room and closed the door. I took her out of the stroller. She explored my room from corner to corner, wall to wall. She didn't get into any trouble. She wanted to see, touch, and smell everything.

I grabbed a book and read for a bit. Betty climbed up and sat in my lap. She seemed to enjoy sitting still. I don't like to sit still for too long. I probably would not make a good bearded dragon!

After a while I put Betty back on the floor. I stood and stretched. Betty raced to my floor pillow. I sometimes liked to sit there to read. Betty sat on it like she sat on her basking rock. Again, she looked like a queen sitting on a throne.

That gave me an idea.

I got my art box and started pulling out supplies.

First I grabbed a piece of yellow paper. I drew a zigzag pattern on it and cut it out. Then I drew circles near the points with my markers. I colored them purple, green, and red, like jewels. I bent the paper into a circle and taped the ends together.

I'd made a mini crown for a mini queen!

I walked over to Betty and sat in front of her. She watched me but didn't move. I carefully placed the crown on her head and held my breath. What would she do?

For a few moments, nothing happened. Then Betty winked at me.

Perfect! I think she liked her new paper crown.

"Your majesty, Queen Betty," I said, bowing my head. "You look amazing. I have never seen a more beautiful bearded dragon. Now just stay still, please. I want to draw your picture."

I reached up to my desk for my sketchbook and a pen. Betty stayed so still that I drew three pictures of her wearing her crown. In the last picture, I drew her sitting on a throne.

I loved having Betty at our house. I was learning a lot about bearded dragons. I almost forgot that we were her foster family, not her forever family.

# CHAPTER 5

# A Forever Home

About an hour later, Dad knocked on my bedroom door. Together we put Betty back in her tank. She climbed on the rock and basked under the lamp.

"Let's make our favorite bearded dragon some lunch," Dad said.

We walked into the kitchen just as Mom was hanging up the phone.

"Guess what?" she asked with a smile. She moved her eyebrows up and down.

I knew that look. My heart dropped into my stomach.

"No!" I said. "It's too soon for Betty to be adopted! We haven't even had her for a full weekend yet."

I was always happy when our foster pets got adopted. Finding forever homes for them was the best. We usually got to keep them longer than a weekend, though.

Mom nodded. "I know. I'm sorry, Kaita," she said. "A family is coming in a few minutes. They really want to adopt her."

My face felt hot. "Did they already talk to Joss?" I asked. "They have to talk to Joss first. She has to decide if they're a good fit for Betty."

I wanted to ask how the family could be so sure they wanted Betty. They didn't know her. Then again I didn't really know her either. She'd lived with us barely two days!

"Yes, Joss spoke to them," Mom said. She smiled again.

Wasn't Mom worried? Why was she smiling so much? She looked like she had a secret. I turned my head up at her, like Betty did with me. Maybe Mom was just happy that Betty was getting a forever family.

*Yip! Yip! Yip!* The family was here.

Ollie ran to the back door. That was strange. Why were these people coming to our back door instead of our front door? Usually only family and good friends came to the back door.

"Kaita, can you please get the door?" Mom asked.

I nudged Ollie to the side and swung open the door. When I saw who was standing there, I grinned.

"Hannah!" I said.

Hannah smiled one of the biggest smiles I'd ever seen. Her dad and mom were with her.

"Wait," I said. "Are *you* adopting Betty?"

Hannah clapped her hands. "We are!" she cried.

Mrs. Miller started to laugh. "Hannah has enjoyed helping you with your foster pets, Kaita," she said. "You know I'm allergic to fur. That's why we can't have furry pets in our house."

"The great news is, Betty has no fur, so we can adopt her!" Hannah said. "Isn't that awesome?"

Ollie yipped and wagged his tail. Oops! Ollie has fur! Mom quickly scooped him up and put him in my bedroom.

Dad and I led Hannah and her parents to the guest room. We all stood around Betty's tank.

"See how pretty she is?" Hannah said.

"I think she looks like a queen," Mrs. Miller said.

"That's what I think too," I said. I ran to get my sketchbook and the crown from my room. I showed the drawings and the crown to the Millers.

"Queen Betty!" I said. "Hannah, you can have her crown. You can use my doll stroller too."

Dad took Betty out of her tank. He put her on Hannah's shoulder.

"She seems very gentle," Mrs. Miller said, rubbing Betty's nose.

Mr. Miller nodded. "I think we found ourselves a new pet!"

"This is going to be great," I said to Hannah.

"I know!" Hannah said. "When I come to your house, we can play with Ollie."

"And when I go to your house, we can play with Betty!" I said.

Perfect!

Mrs. Miller looked closely at Betty's tank. "I hope we can take good care of her," she said. "We don't know very much about bearded dragons."

"You have everything you need for her in her tank," I said. "Betty likes to bask on the rock. She likes climbing the branch. She loves green beans and wax worms."

"You sure know a lot about Betty," Mrs. Miller said.

I thought back to Friday. When Betty first came to us, I didn't know anything about bearded dragons. I learned a lot, though, in two days!

"You will all be Betty experts very soon," I said.

Betty found her forever home with my best friend. I was so happy! I couldn't wait to find out what our next foster pet would be!

# Think About It!

1. What are some things that Kaita does to help care for Betty?
2. What are three things that Betty likes to do?
3. Betty needs a heat lamp to help keep her warm. Ollie does not. What are two other ways that Betty and Ollie are not alike?

# Draw It! Write It!

1. Draw a picture of how you would design Betty's tank. Don't forget the special light so she can warm up. Be sure to have a shady side too, so she can cool down.
2. Pretend you are Kaita's best friend, Hannah. Write a letter to Kaita about why you want to adopt Betty.

# Glossary

**adopt**—to take and raise as one's own

**allergic**—having a physical reaction to something in the environment, such as animals, dust, or certain foods

**bask**—to lie in an area of warmth and light usually created by the sun

**dachshund**—a type of dog with a long body and short legs

**ectotherm**—a creature that needs to use its surroundings to warm up or cool down

**expert**—a person with great skill or a lot of understanding in something

**foster**—to give care and a safe home for a short time

**futon**—a thin, cotton-filled mattress used on the floor or in a wooden frame for sleeping

**swivel**—to turn in any direction around a central point

**veterinarian**—a doctor trained to take care of animals; also called a vet

# Be Your Own Furry Foster Family

Pet foster families take care of all kinds of pets: dogs, cats, rabbits, lizards . . . even ponies! A foster family gives an in-need animal a safe place to live until a forever home can be found.

How do you become a foster family, and what's the experience like? Author Debbi Michiko Florence did some research and also asked a real-life Kaita for tips. While Story Kaita and Real-Life Kaita have their differences—one is Japanese American and in third grade, while the other is half Korean American, half European American and in fifth grade—they both love animals and are experts at fostering pets.

# How do you become a pet foster family?

**Get permission.** Talk to the adults in your family first. Make sure everyone wants to foster.

**Find a local pet-rescue organization.** Research on the computer, at the library, or by asking local veterinarians for help finding a pet-rescue group in your area.

**Fill out an application.** You might also need to have an in-person interview and a home visit. The rescue organization will want to be sure you can give a pet good care.

**Prepare your home and pets.** You might need to have a room just for foster pets, so they feel safe. If you have other pets, make sure their shots are up-to-date. The rescue organization will take care of vet visits, food, and other needed items for the foster pet.

# What's it like to foster?

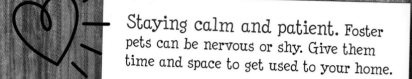

Staying calm and patient. Foster pets can be nervous or shy. Give them time and space to get used to your home.

Paying attention. Every foster pet acts differently and needs different kinds of care. One pet might love to be around the family all the time. Another might want to be left alone.

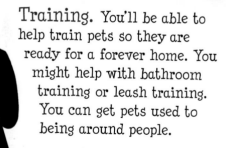

Training. You'll be able to help train pets so they are ready for a forever home. You might help with bathroom training or leash training. You can get pets used to being around people.

**Having fun.** Pet fostering can be a lot of work, but it can bring a lot of joy too! Play! Have fun! Enjoy learning all about your new foster pets.

Real-Life Kaita and her dog Ollie

**Matchmaking.** As a foster family, you'll get to know the pets well. You'll be able to help match them to the perfect forever families.

**Saying goodbye.** It's OK to feel sad when you say goodbye to your foster pets. But remember, you are saving lives by giving them a safe, loving home. And you're making them and their forever families very happy.

# About the Author

**Debbi Michiko Florence** writes books for children in her writing studio, The Word Nest. She is an animal lover with a degree in zoology and has worked at a pet store, the Humane Society, a raptor rehabilitation center, and a zoo. She is the author of two chapter book series: Jasmine Toguchi (FSG) and Dorothy & Toto (Picture Window Books). A third-generation Japanese American and a native Californian, Debbi now lives in Connecticut with her husband, a rescue dog, a bunny, and two ducks.

# About the Illustrator

**Melanie Demmer** is an illustrator and designer based out of Los Angeles, California. Originally from Michigan, she graduated with a BFA in illustration from the College for Creative Studies and has been creating artwork for various apparel, animation, and publishing projects ever since. When she isn't making art, Melanie enjoys writing, spending time in the great outdoors, iced tea, scary movies, and taking naps with her cat, Pepper.

# Go on all four fun, furry foster adventures!

Apple and Annie, the Hamster Duo

by Debbi Michiko Florence
Illustrated by Melanie Demmer

Betty the Bearded Dragon

by Debbi Michiko Florence
Illustrated by Melanie Demmer

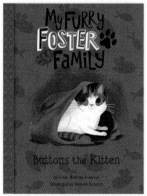

Buttons the Kitten

by Debbi Michiko Florence
Illustrated by Melanie Demmer

Truman the Dog

by Debbi Michiko Florence
Illustrated by Melanie Demmer

## Only from Capstone!